.50

friend dog

friend dog

arnold adoff

pictures by
troy howell

j.b. lippincott
new york

dog

    you
      are my friend
and
      i
      am your
          friend
dog

we are for
each
     other

last spring

            you found me   in the back field
            and i
                    found you
the wild dogs
had
        used your ear   to chew a message

                                    stay
                                    away

we took you to the vet

for shots and healing creams
                              and put you
                              in   a   box
beside the washing machine
            where it was
                        warm

you dreamed your fighting
                chasing
                        dreams

big sister and mama
            and   papa

and me   worked hard on afternoons
      to
            build your run   with a wire fence
                              around   it

            your house with shingles
                        on the roof

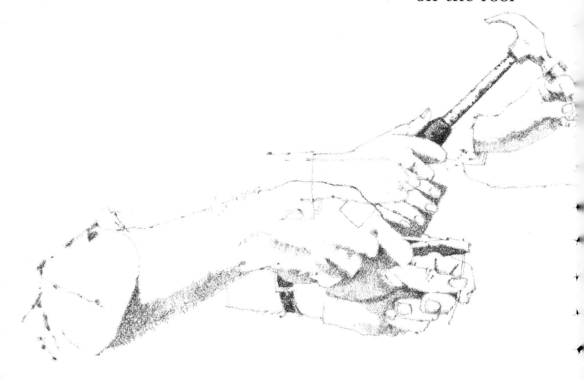

inside your house

                dishes and bowls
                          and
               rawhide chewing
                       bones
an old
   toy turtle   that beeped
                  when you bit
                   his head

a pillow for your bed

friend   and   dog

                                    because
you are both

and they
     are both the same
that
     is
  your
name

dog

        you
        are so black
your
        coat
        your
        coat
                is black

inside the hair
            you
            are
                    blue

dog

     you
     are so smart
sometimes
         you
          are
girl
         and
sometimes

i can be dog

when we are sitting on that flat
rock

and you look at me   and i look
at you
i know we are talking
to each other

i just speak
for us both

my job

      to bring fresh water   and food
      new
      straw
      for the inside
      of your house

your job
      to eat and drink
               and grow   strong
      to
        sleep safe and warm
        through the cold
               night

            dream right

with first light

                          sparrows

and starlings

                  visit

your

bowl

       and fuss

              over

             crumbs

friend dog

        even in this winter time
your morning
        bark will bring me
                out
             of bed
for my breakfast
        and
your
walk

jumping

                into bowls
is your
            best thing

and warm
               wet licks
                        on
                        my
cold
face

dog

you
 are
    too
    low
to   the
  ground
    for
    the
 high
snow

    too
slow
   for
   the
long
race

mama says

if i travel far   and put you down
you
can
go a thousand miles
to find me

and
our
place

we can take you
out

around the yard
where you can
see your run
and your
house
and we can practice
staying
close
when i take off the leash

the run

the house   the bowls of food and water
the
    fresh straw   my hugs and your hurt
                ear
                    are telling
                            you
        there is no
        better
            place   stay near

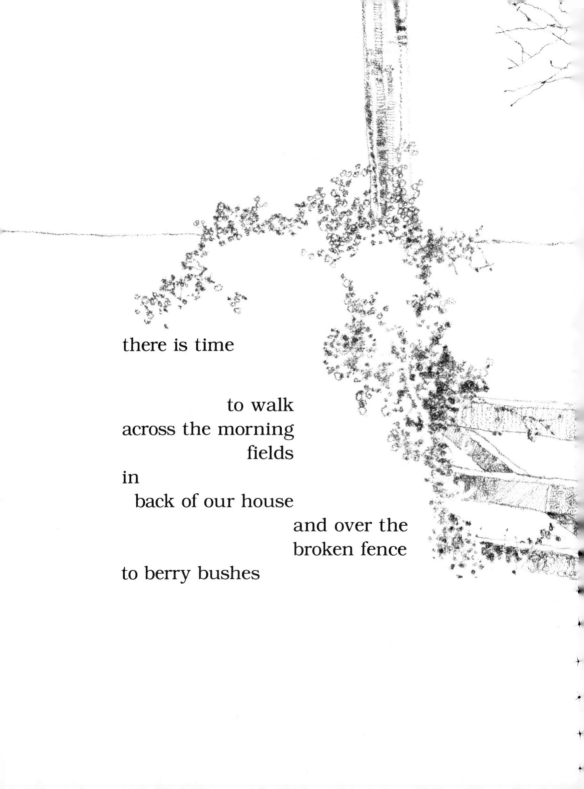

there is time

        to walk
across the morning
          fields
in
  back of our house
         and over the
       broken fence
to berry bushes

our big feet

                    spoil
any surprise
and
the pheasant runs
                    and
                    flie

                              s

into the hole

                    you are
all nose
and noise
and
      i can only see your
        bright red
        christmas collar
        and your dancing
                      tail
            and
            one rabbit
              running
            out
            his
        back
        door

in back
      of our back field

the
    wild dogs
run
    in a
    wild
    pack
      through december cornstalks
          to the broken fence

they hear our noise
and see the
        rabbit
and see
    us both on the shining
          snow

they look mean and hungry

when their leader barks
                              and
                         howls
and looks our
           way
                     we know he cannot
                              be a
                                   friend

if he is calling your name
     he
           only wants to taste
                                   your ear
                                   again

dog
     stay
near

here

is a broken branch   that i can swing
so hard
and fling into the pack

together
we can bark and howl   ourselves
and shout
go away

go way
go way

get b a c
k

and run fast for our yard

then we are safe

another morning   another day
and
    i can drink and watch you
        drink
and
    i can brush your
           coat
and
hug so hard

i draw two cardboard medals

                        shaped like hearts

for
our brave deed   and running speed
             and color them
                        red
        for courage

i pin one to your collar
      and
stick one in
        my
    hat

i pat you on the head

                        you lick
                        your
                                lick

                                    s

and we are a team

        we watch the yard and
                            house
            and listen for the
                            sounds
            of rabbits
                    and
        running
                dogs
                and play a game
                    with sticks
            you teach me
                        new
                        tricks

dog

      you
      are my friend
and
      i
      am your
              friend
dog

we are for
each
      other

For Leigh, Jaime, Fluffy, Essex,
Pepper, and old Friend Dog

Library of Congress Cataloging in Publication Data

Adoff, Arnold.
  Friend dog.

  SUMMARY: A girl relates how she got her dog and
the activities they share.
  1. Dogs—Juvenile poetry.   2. Children's poetry,
American. [1. Dogs—Poetry.   2. American poetry]
I. Howell, Troy.   II. Title.
PS3551.D66F7   1980   811'.54   80-7773
ISBN 0-397-31911-8
ISBN 0-397-31912-6 (lib. bdg.)

    2   3   4   5   6   7   8   9   10